Ytek and the Arctic Orchid

Ytek and the Arctic Orchid

An Inuit Legend / Garnet Hewitt
illustrations / Heather Woodall

Douglas & McIntyre, Vancouver

DOUGLAS & McINTYRE LTD.
1615 VENABLES STREET
VANCOUVER, BRITISH COLUMBIA

CANADIAN CATALOGUING IN PUBLICATION DATA

HEWITT, GARNET, 1939-
          YTEK AND THE ARCTIC ORCHID
          ISBN 0-88894-238-9
          I. WOODALL, HEATHER. II. TITLE.
PS8565.E94Y8   jC813'.54   C80-091197-0
PZ7.H48Yt

TYPESETTING BY DOMINO-LINK WORD AND DATA PROCESSING LTD.
ASSEMBLY BY FREBO STUDIO LIMITED
DESIGN AND JACKET ART BY HEATHER WOODALL
PRINTED AND BOUND IN THE UNITED STATES OF AMERICA

Contents

The Legend

This is a legend about the Inuit and the vast area of Arctic land where they once lived in great numbers. Many of their stories have passed down through the ages by storytellers who were responsible for remembering them. Because the Inuit did not have a written language, the date of this legend is uncertain. But it is very old.

The Arctic land in the legend is known to us as the Barrens. It is an endlessly rolling plain without hills or trees, covered with snow in wintertime and in summer dotted with many lakes and streams. For the Inuit of our story it was a land rich with life. In summer there were caribou, hare, fox, weasel, squirrel, and some wolf and brown bear. Birds and waterfowl came north to nest on the Barrens, and the waterways held a great variety of fishes. There were also many flowers, scattered shrubs and great spreads of moss-like lichen on which the caribou herds grazed.

The Inuit were content with their homeland and the simple life it offered. Fish and caribou were their main food during the short summer season. In winter they lived on stored caribou meat almost entirely, for the hard snow and frozen waterways forced all but a few birds and small animals to move south. When the great herds of caribou migrated southward, the Inuit had a large hunt; enough meat would be frozen in their snow caches to feed everyone during the long Arctic winter.

The legend tells of a time when the caribou became less plentiful on the Inuit hunting grounds, and there was not enough in their food caches to feed them through the harsh winter months. It tells of a young Inuit boy named Ytek and his search for an answer to the problem of the vanishing herds.

Ytek was the only son of an aging Inuit shaman named Owljut. As shaman, Owljut was the hunting and spiritual leader of one Inuit camp. Too old and weak to lead the hunt now, Owljut was training Ytek to take his place. It was not usual to have so young a shaman, for Ytek was only twelve years of age, but custom required that Owljut must hand down his power and responsibility to his son.

2

Becoming a shaman would bring Ytek a great deal of honour. But it would also bring a great deal of responsibility and hard work. Much training would be required. Owljut would instruct Ytek in the ways of nature and the hunting skills needed for the camp's survival. He would also teach his son the secrets of the Inuit spirits, so that his leadership would be wise and respectful of nature.

Ytek's most important task in becoming a shaman would be to conquer a Tornrak — a wild spirit. A Tornrak appears often in the form of an animal or bird, sometimes small, sometimes larger than life. If fought and tamed, this spirit would guide and protect Ytek through his difficult tasks as a shaman.

As the legend begins, Ytek has finished most of his training. He must now face his final test of worthiness. He must conquer his unknown Tornrak, alone and far out on the winter Barrens.

The Characters

INUIT

Ytek *(Ee-tek)* — young shaman
Owljut *(Owl-jut)* — old shaman; Ytek's father
Neenoto *(Nee-not-o)* — Ytek's mother
Mikituk *(Mik-ee-tuk)* — Ytek's young sister

SPIRITS

Kaila *(Kay-la)* — First Spirit of the Sky
Tornrak *(Torn-rak)* — a wild but helpful spirit
Hekenjuk *(Hek-en-juk)* — Spirit of the Sun
Tukturak *(Tuk-too-rak)* — leader of the Tuktu Spirits
Eetanu *(Ee-ta-noo)* — young girl; Tuktu Spirit
Akla *(Ak-la)* — Bear-demon Spirit

ANIMALS

Tuktu *(Tuk-too)* — caribou
Gyrfalcon *(Jer-fal-con)* — large bird; Arctic falcon
Ichloa *(Ich-low-a)* — red trout

TORNRAK

"Eee-aaah.   Wheee-oow."

Kaila, First Spirit of the Sky, raged across the empty land. Snow whistled in circles around Ytek's body, and the cold bit at him like teeth. But he did not stir from his sitting position or look up at the sunless sky, for it was best to hide from the anger of Kaila.

The wait for his Tornrak Spirit seemed endless; it had been days since he left the distant camp behind. He had neither food nor shelter, and for protection he clutched only a short bone spear. He was not eager to do battle with his Tornrak, but he wished that it would find him soon, before he perished from the cold. He remembered terrible stories of grown shamans who had never returned from their ordeal. Ytek bit his lip to help him forget his fear and dug deep into his heart for courage. He must not fail his people.

5

Finally the storm calmed and he raised his eyes to the grey horizon. Then he heard a faint call, like the cry of a distant wind, though no wind was blowing. Closer and closer it came, louder and louder. Suddenly from right above came a shriek like that of a tormented beast.

"Screee-eee!"

Every muscle in his body jumped and his heart hung in his throat. He shook his head as the shriek deafened his ears.

"Screee-eee!"

An awesome giant Spirit in the form of a gyrfalcon plunged down on him. Huge talons from its scaly feet pierced through his parka and into his shoulders like hooked knives. The spear fell from his hand and his scream of panic went unheard across the snow. "Aieee-eee!"

Great wings thundered around him, then he was drawn swiftly up into the air. He gasped at the sight above. Never had he imagined so huge a beast. He had met his Tornrak.

The gyrfalcon's black eyes flashed down at him and its jutting beak snapped angrily. Its breast feathers stood out like spears as Ytek kicked his dangling feet helplessly. He knew that strength alone could not save him from this Tornrak. He was terrified.

Owljut's teachings raced through his mind. Weapons, tools, words, chants — he could remember nothing to help him as long as the bird held him in the air. If he could only find a way to make the bird return to earth, he would have a better chance to fight. Instead, it climbed steeply, drawing him higher. As the great wingtips beat down, lashing the air at his sides, Ytek suddenly recalled some of Owljut's words. The old shaman had once talked about the form of a bird's wing and how the closeness of the feathers help a bird to fly. He also told of how its flight would be broken if these feathers were stretched apart. Ytek shook his mitts from his hands and reached out with both arms to grab the long endfeathers of one beating wing. He clutched a fistful of feathers and pulled them apart with all his strength. The pain in his stabbed shoulders shot along his arms, but he held tightly against the upward motion. The wing broke its pace. Wind whistled through the spread feathers as the surprised beast lost its power of flight. Then bird and boy tumbled from the sky.

Down they spun, swiftly and dizzily. They were both helpless creatures of Kaila now. They would both die, thought Ytek, or they would share the promise of two living partners; for this was the way of Kaila.

All at once the ground loomed before them. Ytek let the wing slip from his grasp. Screaming, the Tornrak loosened its hold on the boy and tried to regain flight — but it was too late. The bird landed on its back in an explosion of snow, the deep drifts breaking its fall. Half-dazed, Ytek found himself on the heaving breast. Before the bird could right itself, he threw himself at its head and thrust his arm down the beast's huge throat. The Tornrak choked for breath, slashing the air with its talons.

Ytek suddenly felt the magic of a shaman's power. He was in control of a ferocious Spirit. As the gyrfalcon's eyes begged for pity, he yanked his arm from its throat. Climbing onto its chest, he jumped up and down to shock air back into its lungs, all the while yelling a shaman's chant that would restore the Tornrak's life. Slowly wind hissed back into the giant's lungs. Pulling three black feathers from the Tornrak's chest, Ytek leaped to the ground and stood, waiting fearfully.

Slowly the bird flopped itself over and rose to its feet. Then Ytek called out his own shaman spell. "Great beast of the sky, you are my Tornrak. I have won your spirit in battle, and I have spared your life." He shook the three feathers at the beast's head. "I will carry these as a sign and your spirit will aid me when I call."

A huge leg lifted over Ytek as if to grab him up again. The young shaman swung the feathers at the razor-sharp talons above his head. There was a loud crack and one talon broke off and fell at the boy's feet.

Shocked, the Tornrak drew back. It lifted its wings, darkening the sky above Ytek. Then it rose almost straight up into the air and disappeared from sight as quickly as it had come.

"Do you hear my words?" cried Ytek. "You must heed my shaman's call!"

"Screee-eee."

The reply came faint and long, like the crying of a distant wind.

TUKTU

Ytek lay under caribou furs, recovering from the battle with his Tornrak. His mother, Neenoto, tended to his wounded shoulders, and his young sister, Mikituk, nourished him with food. He was still so weak that he could not speak, and Owljut sat with the camp elders, waiting to hear his story. Young and old came to pay homage. They were happy to have a new shaman and they filled the Inuit camp with singing and celebration.

While Ytek regained his strength he thought about his first duty as their shaman—a journey far across the winter Barrens to find the Tuktu Spirits. The Inuit depended completely on Tuktu (their name for caribou) for their survival. Frozen caches of Tuktu meat provided food during the long winter when there was little game to hunt. Tuktu also provided most of their clothing and tools. Fur hides became tent coverings, blankets and clothing; hides scraped clean of fur became kayak coverings and dog harnesses. Bones and antlers were shaped into knives, tools, needles and frames for sleds and kayaks. Sinews made sewing thread, fat was melted into oil for lamps. Tuktu was the only animal that could meet all their needs; they had found an important use for nearly every part of it.

But Tuktu herds had become small. Every autumn there was less meat to freeze for the winter. Ytek knew that he must travel to the forests south of the Barrens, where Tuktu herds went in the winter to feed. He must discover why Tuktu was deserting the Inuit hunting grounds. And he knew that he must journey alone. He would need the aid of his Tornrak to reach this unfamiliar land, and only he could benefit from its power.

Everyone helped him prepare for his journey. Hunters and elders equipped Ytek with the best sled and weapons. Strong new leather traces were made for harnessing his dog team, and even the little children helped by fattening the strongest dogs for the long trip. Neenoto fashioned a special belt to carry his three black feathers and talon—his shaman amulets. They were so big that Ytek wore the belt over his shoulder with the amulets hung high on his back. His young friends shared their rations of dried meat for his travel, and bones for the dogs. At last everything was ready. Mikituk bundled the food carefully and packed it on the sled.

All gathered to wish the young shaman a successful quest. Children bounced with excitement because Ytek would venture farther than they had known any Inuit to go before. Mothers with babies peeking from their parka hoods smiled hopefully, thinking of fresh food for their families. "Return soon," Neenoto pleaded. "Little meat remains in the caches and we soon must live on small ptarmigan and hare."

"I will be swift," Ytek replied. "My sled will return with food from Tuktu."

"Your journey will be in the long winter night," spoke Owljut. "May Hekenjuk, Spirit of the Sun, be with you in thought to keep your courage warm."

"Hekenjuk will not be in the sky," replied Ytek, "but I will travel with the courage of your teachings."

Then Owljut pointed to the sky. "Tuktu is in the place of trees now, far from the Inuit. I know that place only in stories of my father's father." He reached out to the amulets on his son's back. "This giant Spirit—it will serve you well. It will take you where other hunters dare not follow. Great wings will speed you when your dogs grow tired. Keen eyes will be your seeing in the long dark sky."

Owljut helped young hunters harness the anxious dogs. Ytek placed his hunting tools and snowshoes in the sled. He called to the lead dog as he stepped onto the sled runners. Soon his people were far behind.

Days passed and nothing in the endless flat snow marked his progress. Hekenjuk was only a brief glimmer above the lip of the horizon each day and then sank quickly. The diminishing pack of food was his best measure of the distance he had travelled. When the food was gone he hunted ptarmigan and hare to feed himself and his dogs, but they were scarce.

Like all Inuit hunters in a hurry, he built only a low snow wall to lie behind when he slept. This protected him from the sharp wind, and his double winter parka of Tuktu furs kept him warm with his own body heat. The dogs dug into the snow and curled their thick tails over their tender noses.

One night Ytek was awakened by a strange and frightening dream. He dreamed that as he journeyed, he came upon large crimson spots of blood that marked a trail in the snow. The spots led him to a frozen lake, but when he started to cross it, the ice gave way. He awoke as he was falling. Troubled by the dream that seemed so real, Ytek sat for a long time puzzling over its meaning. He was filled with doubts. He had hoped to reach the southern forests without help, but lack of food made him weak and his dogs were now running slower and slower. It was time to summon his Tornrak.

He stood up. Removing the amulet belt from his shoulder he began to swirl it in a slow circle over his head. The long feathers and talon whistled through the air. "Great bird with keen eye and giant wing, show me the way to Tuktu." He paused and listened. Then he began again. "Great bird, there I must go, swift and true. My people hunger. My sled must return to camp heavy with food."

As before, the Tornrak's reply came at first faint and distant. Then it grew so loud that the stars seemed to tremble. The dogs scrambled up nervously from beneath the snow. Ytek harnessed them hastily and they strained at their leads, ready for his command.

"Screee-eee!"

Like magic, huge wings appeared above his head. The thought of his first meeting with the Tornrak made a shiver run down Ytek's back. Did the beast know it was not to harm him now? The great bird swooped, causing a flurry of snow to swirl around Ytek. Then it rose and turned northward, flapping low across the land.

At first it flew slowly, almost in slow motion. The harness traces snapped tight even without Ytek's signal, as the dogs took chase. Then the Tornrak's speed quickened and the dogs ran to keep pace. Ytek clung firmly to the rails of the sled as it rocked crazily over drifts. He was puzzled that the Tornrak was leading them north rather than south where the Tuktu herds wintered. But they were moving so fast he had no time to wonder and could only cling desperately to the racing sled.

ORCHID

For a long time they raced across the snow, almost as if the bird were pulling them with its own magic power. When it was too dark to sight the bird, they were guided by its call and by the path its powerful wingbeat churned in the snow. Suddenly the Tornrak seemed to dive into the ground and vanish. The dogs slowed down until the sled came to a stop near the place where the bird had disappeared. Ytek scanned the horizon. He could see nothing, not even wing marks in the snow. Then he saw a small dark spot ahead and urged the dogs forward once more.

As they drew up to the spot, Ytek jumped from the runners in surprise. There in the frozen snow grew a beautiful crimson flower. Its tender petals were open in full bloom, seemingly untouched by the bitter wind. He could scarcely believe his eyes. Pulling off his mitts he touched the blossom—it was real. Then ahead he noticed another flower. Remembering his dream now, he drove the team forward in excitement. There was another crimson flower, and another, forming a trail across the frozen land.

Before he noticed it, they had sped onto a circle of ice. The dogs' feet slid out from under them and they skidded on their bellies across the slippery surface. While the animals tried to regain their footing, Ytek stepped cautiously from the sled's runners and looked around him. They were in the middle of the ice circle with the strange crimson blooms growing around its rim. Ytek shuffled across the ice and knelt before one of the flowers. Uncertain if he was awake or dreaming, he bent his head and touched one of the velvet-soft petals with his lips. At the moment his lips met the petal, the entire ice circle trembled. He sprang to his feet as deep cracks shot across the surface of the ice like jagged lightning. The dogs whined in fear and Ytek instinctively turned to the sled to lead them away from harm.

Creee-eek!   Craaa-aack!

With a loud noise the middle of the circle splintered into a slippery funnel. Ytek was slammed into the sled among the team of frightened, yelping dogs. He grabbed his amulet belt from his shoulder and began to yell a shaman spell, but it was too late. In a final thunder of shattering ice, his helpless scream followed him into the depths below.

"Aieee-eee!"

Ytek shook the numbness from his head. To his surprise, no water gurgled into his lungs and he saw no black horror of icy depths. Instead a warm breeze blew across his face and soft green lichen tickled the end of his nose. Carefully he raised himself from the patch of ground on which he lay, feeling each bone and muscle to discover that nothing was broken or even bruised. But all around him were huge splinters of ice, piled so high that he could see only the hole through which they had fallen. And past that hole, which was almost within reach, he could see the dim sky of the world they had left above. The unbroken ice spread like a roof over another world below. The whimpering of his dogs brought Ytek to his feet. They too were unharmed, and he used his bone knife to cut their tangled harnesses. Then he climbed to the top of the ice pile to see where he was.

Ytek stood on the peak of a hill. Below lay a magical valley. He could see hills colourful with tiny flowers and lichen, and sparkling lakes of blue and emerald. Yet there was a mystery: summer and winter were both here. Some hills and trees were covered in fresh, deep snow; others were green and bright with summer flowers. Even the steep slopes that enclosed the valley shared mixed seasons.

On the hills and in the valley were the tall pine trees that Ytek had heard about but never before seen. They too were caught in a pattern of summer and winter; some branches hung heavy with snow, others stretched out fresh and green. The ice crystals of the frozen roof-sky magnified Hekenjuk's dim light and turned it into rainbows of glittering colour on the valley below.

Ytek was eager to get a closer look at the unfamiliar pines. He started off down the hill, his team of dogs at his heels. As they moved, they startled squirrel, ptarmigan and fox, and when a family of Arctic hare bounded from a flower patch, the dogs chased them to the valley bottom. At last Ytek stood beneath the towering trees, so huge that he found himself comparing them with his giant Tornrak. They grew at the edge of a lake which was so quiet and clear that he could see red trout in its depths. "Ichloa," he declared to the dogs, pointing to the fish. He was happy to discover things of his own world.

Just then the sound of singing drifted along the pebbled shore. Commanding the dogs to lie still, he walked softly behind the line of trees. When the singing was close, he stepped silently from beneath the low boughs and onto the beach. A few steps away, a young girl was gathering twigs. She was bent far over the ground, intent on her work. The words of her song were in the Inuit language and she was dressed in Inuit clothing. In his surprise, Ytek could not speak or move. The girl reached his feet, then straightened up in shock, her armful of twigs scattering to the ground.

MAGIC VALLEY

After a long startled stare, the girl spoke first. "You are not of our camp."

Ytek's heart was pounding and his throat felt so tight that he could not answer.

The girl tried again. "My name is Eetanu."

Ytek forced his lips to move. "They call me Ytek." His voice was so low it was almost a whisper.

"Where is the camp of your people?" she asked. "How did you find this place?"

When Ytek realized that Eetanu was as surprised as he was, he relaxed and his words came freely.

22

"My people's camp is far away. I was on a long hunt and became lost." The girl listened with a puzzled look. "I followed a large gyrfalcon to the crimson blossoms in the snow," he explained. "When I touched my lips to one the ice broke below me. I thought the Water Spirit would swallow me in anger. I think I am alive. But I am not sure if I am in my own world or in another."

Eetanu tossed her long black braids. "How did you know about the secret of tasting the magic Orchid to enter our valley?" she asked. "No stranger has ever come before . . . and all the Inuit camps are far to the south."

"To the south!" cried Ytek. "But then the gyrfalcon has led me astray. I was searching for the southern forests where Tuktu winters, for I must talk with the Spirit of Tuktu.

Eetanu's face lit up. "Spirit of Tuktu? Then you are not lost, Ytek. This is not the winter place of Tuktu, but it *is* the place of the First Spirit of Tuktu. This is the secret valley of Tukturak."

At the sound of the word Tukturak, Ytek's heart beat faster. Owljut had told him of the First Spirit of Tuktu, the very first Tuktu that Kaila had placed on the world. But why had his father, wise with many secrets, not told him of this place?

"Come to our camp," Eetanu said. "You must need food and rest. There you will meet Tukturak, who can answer all your questions."

Ytek called to his dogs and they came scrambling along the stony shore. Eetanu led them beside the lake and up the bank until they came upon the camp of hide tents. People, alerted by the noisy dogs, came forward to greet the young stranger. As they drew close, a tall, strong man appeared from a tent opening. His hands held a shaman's rod with a belt of amulets strung down its length. His face showed the wisdom of many ages. But his most striking feature was his hair. It fell in two long silver braids over his shoulders and down the front of his parka. Its colour was like that of a shimmering winter moon.

"This is Ytek," said Eetanu. "He comes to talk with the Spirit of Tuktu."

Tukturak smiled at Ytek as he pointed to the large amulets on the boy's shoulders. "You are young for a shaman. You are young for the powerful Tornrak of those feathers. You must have an important purpose, to hold so much power. We will talk of this purpose as you rest and eat." He raised his rod, motioning to have fur mats set out on the ground and pointed Ytek to one opposite his own. All the valley dwellers crowded in eagerly. The young ones drew close, while those who had begun to prepare a feast of welcome waited for the stranger to speak. Only the hungry dogs seemed uninterested as they crunched on their food.

Everyone listened carefully as Ytek told the story of his camp and the journey to the hidden valley. As he spoke he drew with his fingers in the

soft fur of the Tuktu mats to show the direction of his travels. Then he raised his head to ask Tukturak his important question.

"Tuktu herds grow small and migrate far from our camp. There is little food for my people in winter. By spring there will be illness." He paused, remembering his people. "Tukturak, will you tell me why this is?"

Tukturak broke the silence that followed the young shaman's question with a single word.

"Akla."

Ytek shuddered. Owljut had spoken to him of the Demon-Spirit Akla, a terror that every shaman must protect his people from.

Tukturak continued. "This bear-demon has always been known for his fierce appetite. But now Akla kills without need or hunger. The demon slays Tuktu only to marvel at its own power."

An elder spoke. "If it were not for this hidden valley, we too would be in danger of the great bear-demon."

Tukturak explained. "All who dwell in this secret valley are Tuktu Spirits. It is our purpose to guide Tuktu across land that is safe from Akla—land that is now far from your hunting grounds."

"How can you guide Tuktu when you live in the bodies of Inuit?" Ytek asked.

Then Tukturak told Ytek about the magic Arctic Orchid and the secret valley. "There was a time when we lived only in the bodies of Tuktu. But as Akla grew more vicious, it began to prey on us also, the Tuktu Spirits. One winter we had to flee far to the north. Kaila saw that we would die without food or shelter. So Kaila spoke to the Water Spirit. Water Spirit thundered in the lake on which we stood and strange crimson blooms grew suddenly through the ice. When we ate them in hunger, the ice crumbled and we fell into this valley. But as we fell, our bodies took the form of Inuit bodies.

"At first we were puzzled by this change. But we came down into the valley and practised the ways of the Inuit. Then it came to me that Kaila wished us to know how the Inuit live, for the life of Tuktu and the life of the Inuit are like one.

"Now when spring comes to the land above, we wait with kayaks on the big hill. Water Spirit makes the sky ice fall as sudden rain and the winter snows run like rivers. The valley again becomes a lake and we paddle ashore to eat the crimson blooms at its edge. Our bodies return to the form of Tuktu so that we can speed southward and guide the migrating herds."

Ytek's face glowed with amazement. "That is beyond even my father's dreams." Then he began to laugh with joy, for he had learned the secret of Tuktu. Surely if Tukturak had this much power there must be a way of getting winter food for his people.

As the young shaman laughed, Tukturak and the others joined in, and soon they were all rolling about on the fur mats, shaking with merriment. Now it was time for celebration. Women brought great trays of steaming meat. Children tumbled over one another to touch the stranger. Songs and stories rang out and dogs yelped with excitement. Ytek felt as if he were at home among his own people. And all the while Tukturak's words kept ringing in his ears:

"The life of Tuktu and the life of the Inuit are like one."

AKLA

Ytek arose very early the following day. Through the tent opening he could see people preparing a sled with many packs of meat, enough to feed his people through the rest of the winter. When all was ready, the valley dwellers climbed with him to the top of the big hill and stood beneath the ice sky, listening as Tukturak told his plan to the young shaman.

"When we guide the migration north, we will return Tuktu to the Inuit hunting grounds. As soon as we scent the terror of Akla, our herd of Tuktu Spirits will trick the demon into a chase away from your camp. Tuktu can continue safely to your hunting grounds, and with Kaila's help we will escape Akla's claws."

30

Then the group piled up blocks of the fallen ice and helped Ytek climb through the hole, which was still partly open from his fall of the day before. Next they pushed the sled up after him and the packs of meat. Last, each squirming dog was lifted up, while Ytek harnessed them one by one. Finally the boy lay on his stomach at the hole in the ice and called down to his friends below.

"My people will be joyful with the food and the message I bring. We will celebrate the valley beneath the crimson blossoms and the power of Tuktu Spirits."

As he was taking a last look down at the beautiful valley, Eetanu stepped forward and smiled up at him. "Remember the crimson flower that we named the Orchid," she said. "And remember your new Spirit-friends who hide beneath its magic."

Ytek returned her smile. "Whenever the wind sings, I will remember your song on the shore of the emerald lake, Eetanu. And I will watch for you if chance brings you near our hunting grounds as you guide Tuktu." He paused. "But how can I know Tuktu Spirits from Tuktu herds?"

"If fortune brings us near your camp, I too will watch for you, Ytek," said Eetanu. "There is no way you can see our difference, except for Tukturak. His great antlers shine like the silver braids of his hair."

Already the hole in the sky ice had begun filling up to enclose the valley's secret again. Ytek stood alone at the edge of the ice and summoned his Tornrak once more. Its muffled answer came from its hiding place in the valley below, and he watched its giant shadow rise like a great grey ghost through the thick ice. The boy jumped to the sled runners and the dogs plunged off across the land as if they had wings.

Closer and closer to home they sped, travelling day and night. Once more the Tornrak seemed to fill the dogs with tireless speed, and Ytek felt the magic strength returning. His thoughts were on a happy reunion with his people.

Then without warning the Tornrak began to dodge, first left, then right, as if trying to escape a pursuer. While Ytek watched, the bird disappeared overhead with a frightening screech. A fearful trembling of the ground shook the dogs from their feet, crashing the sled into the drifts and dumping Ytek headlong into the snow. The young shaman raised his head and a fearful scent reached his nose. Instinctively he knew what lay ahead.

"Aaaa-rrrgh!"

Akla, the giant bear-demon, towered above him. Ytek gasped. If he had been standing, his head would scarcely reach to the beast's knees. The great head was almost hairless, like a white skull of death; blood-red eyes bulged from their sockets. Four huge fangs gaped from the cavernous mouth, still matted with the hair and flesh of devoured animals.

Ytek lunged for his bow and arrows, but before he could reach them two huge paws darkened the sky and claws like twisted daggers closed around his body. He was scooped into the black hole of the demon's mouth.

"Screee-eee!"

The Tornrak shot from above like an arrow, wings back, beak snarling, talons pointed for battle. Straight for Akla's head it came. The demon opened its great jaws with a roar, ready to fight back, and Ytek spilled to the ground.

Akla's giant paw swung wildly through the air in a rush of wind, but the Tornrak struck first. There was a loud crash of beak against bone, the tear of talon on flesh, a whirlwind of ripped feathers and hair. As the bear-demon staggered backwards, pawing wildly at its attacker, the Tornrak struck again. A roar of pain and rage filled the sky and the bird rose with a thundering swoop of wings, bearing away one of Akla's blood-red eyes. Ytek scrambled out of the way as the giant crashed to the ground beside him.

Akla rolled over and over in the drifts of snow, howling with pain. Finally the Demon-Spirit rose on all fours and lumbered blindly away, its howls echoing across the frozen land.

Ytek struggled to his feet. His muscles ached and his ribs creaked with every breath, but he had escaped serious injury. Slowly he made his way along the sled track, calling his dogs. He found them cowering in a mass of tangled harness and meat packs. When they were strung out again and the sled repacked, Ytek set off again in the direction they had been travelling. His Tornrak was gone, but he knew that he was not too far from home.

SPIRIT FRIENDS

The Inuit were joyful at the sight of their young shaman. As his strength returned, he shared with his people all his marvellous adventures. They squirmed with excitement as he described his strange dream and the wild journey behind his Tornrak. They hung with silent wonder on every word when he described the hidden valley and the Tuktu Spirits. And their teeth clenched and faces twisted in pain with each detail of the battle between the demon Akla and the gyrfalcon. They held a celebration for the Tuktu Spirits and the promise of good hunting to come.

Spring did come, breaking the long winter cold. Rivers ran again, lakes teemed with fish, and birds and animals appeared on the Barrens. Long lines of Tuktu headed north to feed on rich summer lichen, crossing Inuit hunting grounds, as Tukturak had promised.

Summer passed swiftly. One autumn day, Ytek squatted by his father's tent, repairing a kayak. He was so intent on his work that he did not notice a group of his people's hunters running across the plains towards him. Owljut, Neenoto and Mikituk appeared in their tent opening to see what the fuss was about.

Ytek stood up. "What is it that gives you such short wind?" he asked.

"Tuktu!" panted one hunter. He threw up an arm to the horizon behind them.

"But surely you have seen Tuktu before," exclaimed Ytek.

"Only listen!" another hunter said. "We sat resting on a rise of rock, enjoying Hekenjuk's warm light. Suddenly a small herd of Tuktu galloped across our sight. Yet they did not gallop like most Tuktu—they seemed almost to fly over the ground with the speed of birds. When they scented us, they stopped quickly and turned to face us."

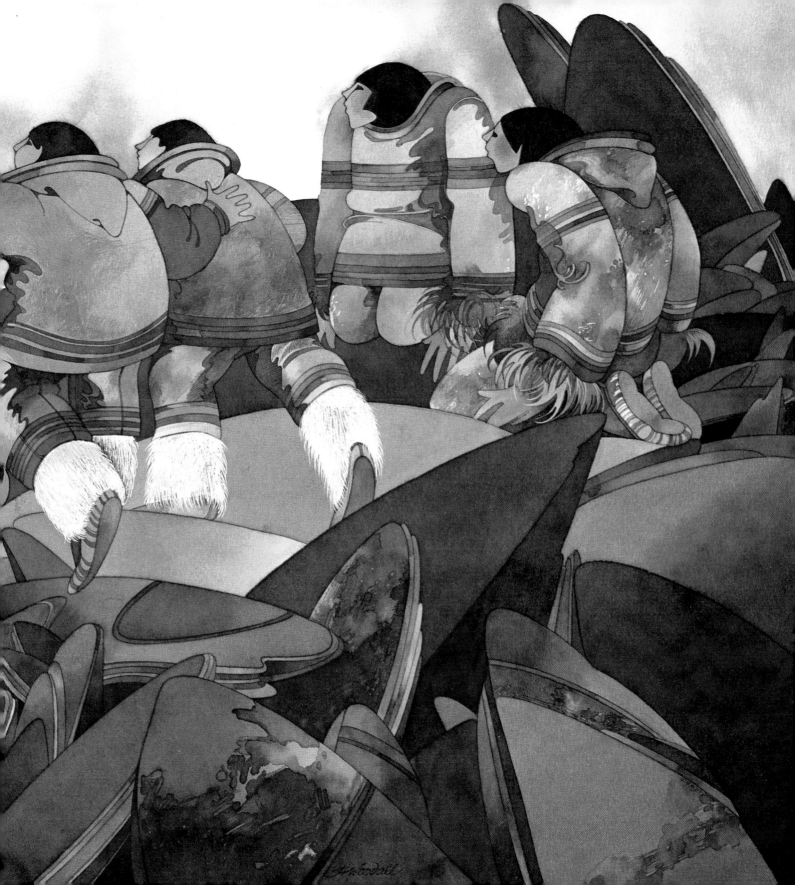

Another hunter took up the story. "Most of the herd halted a short distance away, but a great buck and a young doe climbed the rise to stand before us. They were so close we could have reached out and touched them, but we could only open our mouths in surprise. The buck, Ytek, it was like none I have ever seen before. It stood taller than any other and its huge antlers showed it to be of a great age. But those antlers! They shone silver, like the brightest winter moon. The buck and the doe turned their heads from side to side, as if they were searching for one they knew."

Then a fourth hunter broke in with excitement. "Finally the buck and doe turned back to the waiting herd, and they all galloped off together. They went like the wind and we marvelled at their speed. We couldn't take our eyes off the great buck's silver antlers. They shone in the distance until they vanished over the horizon."

38

Ytek felt a warmth grow in his heart as he listened to every word of the hunters. He recalled the magic flowers and the secret valley, his new Spirit-friends and the long silver braids of Tukturak. And he remembered young Eetanu singing beside the emerald lake.

Wise old Owljut turned to his young shaman son. "Tukturak? Eetanu?" he questioned softly.

Ytek smiled his silent reply.